佩佩家的電腦

豬媽媽正在使用電腦，
她打字打得很快。
今天豬媽媽有好多重要工作
要處理。

豬ㄓㄨ爸ㄅㄚ爸ㄅㄚ在ㄗㄞˋ廚ㄔㄨˊ房ㄈㄤˊ
煮ㄓㄨˇ午ㄨˇ餐ㄘㄢ要ㄧㄠˋ喝ㄏㄜ的ㄉㄜ湯ㄊㄤ。

「爸ㄅㄚ爸ㄅㄚ，」佩ㄆㄟˋ佩ㄆㄟˋ問ㄨㄣˋ：「我ㄨㄛˇ們ㄇㄣ可ㄎㄜˇ以ㄧˇ去ㄑㄩˋ看ㄎㄢˋ
媽ㄇㄚ媽ㄇㄚ打ㄉㄚˇ電ㄉㄧㄢˋ腦ㄋㄠˇ嗎ㄇㄚ？拜ㄅㄞˋ託ㄊㄨㄛ。」
「可ㄎㄜˇ以ㄧˇ，只ㄓˇ要ㄧㄠˋ你ㄋㄧˇ們ㄇㄣ不ㄅㄨ要ㄧㄠˋ打ㄉㄚˇ擾ㄖㄠˇ她ㄊㄚ。」
豬ㄓㄨ爸ㄅㄚ爸ㄅㄚ說ㄕㄨㄛ。

「媽媽，」佩佩問：「喬治和我
可以坐在你的腿上看你工作嗎？」

「可以，只要你們兩個安靜的坐著。」豬媽媽答應。

大約一分鐘之後，佩佩問：
「我們可以用電腦玩
快樂母雞的遊戲嗎？」

豬媽媽說：「等一下可以玩快樂母雞的遊戲，但是現在我必須工作。」

又ㄧㄡˋ過ㄍㄨㄛˋ了ㄌㄜ一ㄧ分ㄈㄣ鐘ㄓㄨㄥ，佩ㄆㄟˋ佩ㄆㄟˋ問ㄨㄣˋ：
「媽ㄇㄚ媽ㄇㄚ，我ㄨㄛˇ們ㄇㄣ可ㄎㄜˇ以ㄧˇ幫ㄅㄤ你ㄋㄧˇ工ㄍㄨㄥ作ㄗㄨㄛˋ嗎ㄇㄚ？」
佩ㄆㄟˋ佩ㄆㄟˋ模ㄇㄛˊ仿ㄈㄤˇ媽ㄇㄚ媽ㄇㄚ在ㄗㄞˋ電ㄉㄧㄢˋ腦ㄋㄠˇ上ㄕㄤˋ打ㄉㄚˇ字ㄗˋ。

「不，佩佩！」
豬媽媽說：「當我
在工作時，你不能
碰電腦。」

「喬治，不行！」佩佩用命令的口氣說：「你絕對不可以這樣。」佩佩按了返回鍵，電腦忽然閃爍一下。

「佩佩，快住手！」豬媽媽說。
「對不起，媽媽。」佩佩說：「我只是想告訴喬治不要亂碰。」

「豬爸爸！」豬媽媽大喊：「我來做午餐，你可以修理電腦嗎？」

「嗯……」豬爸爸說：「我不太擅長這件事。」

「嗯……」豬爸爸按了一個按鍵。

「嗯……」豬爸爸又按了另一個按鍵。

「也許我應該關機再重開……」

豬ㄓㄨ爸ㄅㄚ爸ㄅㄚ把ㄅㄚ電ㄉㄧㄢ腦ㄋㄠ修ㄒㄧㄡ好ㄏㄠ了ㄌㄜ！
「好ㄏㄠ耶ㄧㄝ！ 爸ㄅㄚ爸ㄅㄚ。 」佩ㄆㄟ佩ㄆㄟ歡ㄏㄨㄢ呼ㄏㄨ。

她ㄔㄚ和ㄔㄜ喬ㄑㄧㄠ治ㄓ跳ㄊㄧㄠ上ㄔㄤ跳ㄊㄧㄠ下ㄒㄧㄚ。
「 太ㄊㄞ好ㄏㄠ了ㄌㄜ， 」 豬ㄓㄨ爸ㄅㄚ爸ㄅㄚ微ㄨㄟ笑ㄒㄧㄠ，
「 看ㄎㄢ來ㄌㄞ我ㄨㄛ是ㄕ修ㄒㄧㄡ電ㄉㄧㄢ腦ㄋㄠ的ㄉㄜ專ㄓㄨㄢ家ㄐㄧㄚ呢� ！ 」

「爸爸，」佩佩問：「我們可以玩電腦遊戲——快樂母雞嗎？媽媽說等一下我們可以玩。」

「而現在已經是等一下了。」佩佩說。

「那麼，」豬爸爸想了一下，
「好吧。」豬爸爸啟動了
快樂母雞遊戲。

「呵ㄏㄜ，呵ㄏㄜ，呵ㄏㄜ！」當ㄉㄤ佩ㄆㄟ佩ㄆㄟ和ㄏㄜ喬ㄑㄧㄠ治ㄓ玩ㄨㄢ快ㄎㄨㄞ樂ㄌㄜ母ㄇㄨ雞ㄐㄧ遊ㄧㄡ戲ㄒㄧ時ㄕ，豬ㄓㄨ爸ㄅㄚ爸ㄅㄚ大ㄉㄚ笑ㄒㄧㄠ。

「齁ㄏㄡ！」當ㄉㄤ豬ㄓㄨ媽ㄇㄚ媽ㄇㄚ走ㄗㄡ進ㄐㄧㄣ房ㄈㄤ間ㄐㄧㄢ時ㄕ，她ㄊㄚ說ㄕㄨㄛ：「我ㄨㄛ看ㄎㄢ到ㄉㄠ電ㄉㄧㄢ腦ㄋㄠ修ㄒㄧㄡ好ㄏㄠ啦ㄌㄚ！」

Peppa Pig's Family Computer

Mummy Pig is working on the family computer.
She is typing very fast. Mummy Pig has a lot
of important work to do today.

Daddy Pig is in the kitchen making soup for lunch.

"Daddy?" Peppa asks. "Can we go and watch Mummy on the computer, please?"
"Yes, as long as you don't disturb her," Daddy Pig says.

"Mummy?" Peppa asks. "Can George and I sit on your lap and watch you work?"

About a minute later, Peppa asks, "Can we play the Happy Mrs Chicken game on the computer?"

Mummy Pig says, "We can play Happy Mrs Chicken later. But now I have to work."

Another minute later, Peppa asks, "Mummy? Can we help you work?" Peppa taps away at the computer like Mummy Pig.

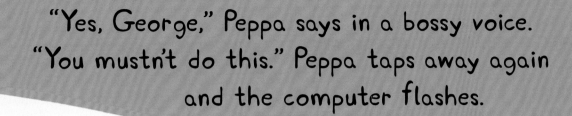

"Yes, George," Peppa says in a bossy voice.
"You mustn't do this." Peppa taps away again
and the computer flashes.

"Peppa! Stop!"
Mummy Pig says.
"Sorry, Mummy," Peppa says.
"I was just showing George
what not to do."

"Daddy Pig!" Mummy calls. "Can you mend the computer while I finish the lunch?"
"Uh . . ." Daddy Pig says. "I'm not very good with these things."

"Hmmm . . ." Daddy Pig
pushes a button.

"Mmmm . . ." Daddy Pig
pushes another button.

"Maybe if I switch it off
and switch it on again . . ."

Daddy Pig has mended the computer!
"Hooray, Daddy!" shouts Peppa.

She and George jump up and down.
"Yes," Daddy Pig smiles. "I am a bit of
an expert at these things."

"Daddy," Peppa asks. "Can we play that computer game, Happy Mrs Chicken? Mummy said we could play it later," Peppa says. "And now it's later!"

"Well," Daddy Pig thinks for a moment,
"OK then." Daddy Pig starts
the Happy Mrs Chicken game.

"Ho, ho, ho!" Daddy Pig laughs as Peppa
and George play Happy Mrs Chicken.
"Snort!" Mummy Pig says as she comes into the room.
"I see the computer is working again!"